W9-AYR-228

The Prince, the Cook, and the Cunning King

by Terry Deary

illustrated by Helen Flook

PICTURE WINDOW BOOKS
Minneapolis, Minnesota

Managing Editor: Catherine Neitge
Story Consultant: Terry Flaherty
Page Production: Tracy Davies
Creative Director: Keith Griffin
Editorial Director: Carol Jones

First American edition published in 2006 by
Picture Window Books
5115 Excelsior Boulevard
Suite 232
Minneapolis, MN 55416
877-845-8392
www.picturewindowbooks.com

First published in Great Britain by
A & C Black Publishers Limited
37 Soho Square, London W1D 3QZ
Text copyright © 2003 Terry Deary
Illustrations copyright © 2003 Helen Flook

Library of Congress Cataloging-in-Publication Data
Deary, Terry.
  The prince, the cook, and the cunning king / by Terry Deary; illustrated
by Helen Flook.
      p. cm. — (Read it! chapter books) (Historical tales)
  Summary: The niece of King Henry VII of England infiltrates the
servants' quarters to find out if one of the kitchen helpers is trying to
become king.
  Includes bibliographical references.
  ISBN 1-4048-1298-9 (hardcover)
  1. Great Britain—History—Henry VII, 1485–1509—Juvenile fiction.
[1. Great Britain—History—Henry VII, 1485–1509—Fiction.] I. Flook,
Helen, ill. II. Title. III. Series.
  PZ7.D3517Pri 2005
  [Fic]—dc22   2005007216

Table of Contents

This book is dedicated to the memory of Perkin Warbeck, another young man who claimed Henry VII's throne, but who paid for it with his life.—Terry Deary

The Cold Kitchen

We stood at the palace door and shivered. The wind was wintry, the gray walls gloomy. I was afraid. My mother was just about to knock for a second time when the door was tugged open and I found myself looking into the palace kitchen.

A dozen dirty faces stared at me. The servants were sitting around a large table with wooden bowls in front of them.

"Shut the door!" someone moaned. "It's cold!"

My mother pushed me into the kitchen ahead of her, and the door slammed behind us with a boom like the sound of doom.

The dozen pairs of eyes followed us into the cold kitchen.

There was a huge fireplace with copper pots, iron pans hanging down alongside dead rabbits and geese, and a shriveled side of bacon. In that fireplace, a miserable fire smoked under a small black pot full of pale and pitiful porridge.

A man lifted the pot off the fire and placed it on the table.

The servants passed it around and spooned out the watery mess. They ate it silently.

The man turned to look at me. He was the fattest man I'd ever seen. Folds of fat almost hid his little, watery eyes, and his neck was like a bull's. When he smiled, his teeth were yellow-green and broken. His greasy apron smelled nearly as bad as his breath. He put a hard hand under my chin and tilted my head up. "So, you're the new kitchen maid?"

"This is Eleanor—Ellie," my mother said. "Say hello to Cook, Ellie."

"Hello to Cook, Ellie," I muttered.

The clatter of wooden spoons in the sloppy food stopped. Twelve servants at the table held their breath. Cook's eyes almost vanished in a scowl. Then he grinned.

"A lively lass, eh? That's a change from this miserable lot!" he said, looking round at the servants who started eating again.

He nodded to my mother. "Leave her with me and I'll take care of her."

My mother left the bundle with my spare clothes and hurried to the door. She opened it and looked back, worried.

"Shut the door!" someone moaned. "It's cold!"

She left me. Alone.

The cook looked around the table. "Lambert Simnel," he hissed.

A boy rose to his feet. He was as thin as the porridge in the pot and twice as pale.

"Yes, Cook?" he said, and he shivered.

"Look after young Ellie. Show her where she sleeps. Show her what to do."

"Yes, Cook."

The boy looked back longingly at his half-full bowl of mush. He left the bench and moved toward me, walking almost sideways like a crab. As he passed Cook, the fat man lashed out at Lambert, and the boy ducked.

"He didn't do anything!" I cried.

Cook turned his fat face on me. His lips curled back to show those green teeth.

"Lambert has been a wicked, wicked boy, haven't you, Lambert?"

"Yes, Cook."

"He doesn't deserve a smack on the head!" I said and my face was hot in that cold kitchen.

"No," Cook said softly. Then a dirty finger prodded me in the shoulder, and he exploded with stinking breath in my face. "He deserves an ax on the back of his scrawny neck!"

Suddenly, he picked up a meat-ax from a table and shook it wildly. "He deserves to be executed. Don't you, Lambert?"

"Yes, Cook," the miserable boy murmured.

"Now take her to the room over the stables and show her where she'll be sleeping."

Lambert nodded, gave me a quivering smile, picked up my bundle, and nodded for me to follow him. I stopped at the door and looked back to see one of the servants emptying Lambert's porridge bowl.

"I have to sleep *here*?" I asked Lambert.

He nodded and dropped my bundle onto a pile of straw in the loft.

"Sleep on the straw," he said. "Use the blanket to cover you. It's warm with the horses below you in the stable."

I was staring at my bed.

"The straw moved," I whispered.

Lambert laughed. "That'll just be a rat. I have a special rat friend," he said.

Suddenly he darted to the top of the stairs and looked down. "People listen at doors here, you know?" He scuttled back to me. "I call my rat Henry. After the king!"

"The king would be furious, if he knew," I said.

"The king is the biggest rat of all," he said wildly. "Why do you think everyone in the palace is so miserable? Because the king is so mean. We eat the cheapest food. Even his wife, Queen Elizabeth, is made to patch her dresses. She has tin buckles on her shoes when a queen should have silver!"

"Cook looks fat enough," I said.

Lambert dashed to the top of the steps and back again. "He steals the king's food.

If we did it, we'd be whipped. But Cook has the key to the pantry."

I sat down on the straw. Lambert was right. It was warm enough.

"Why did Cook call you wicked?"

Lambert ran to the top of the stairs and back for the third time. He spoke quickly. "King Henry stole the crown of England. The real king should be Prince Edward, but he was locked in the Tower of London by King Henry Tudor."

"I've heard the story. He's still locked away there, isn't he?"

Lambert shook his head so hard I thought it would fall off on to the rat-filled straw. "Edward escaped!" he squeaked.

"How do you know, Lambert?" I asked quietly.

"Because it's me! I'm Edward, Earl of Warwick. I'm the real king of England!"

The Midnight Meeting

That day, I learned my duty as kitchen maid. I scrubbed pans with sand, and I swept the floor. I made bread till my arms ached, and I carried buckets of water until my shoulders were numb.

We had bread and cheese for lunch, but Cook didn't eat with us. He disappeared into the pantry for two hours and came out with food dribbling down his chin, looking sleepy. Then it was time to make the evening meal for the king and his court.

Cook breathed over me. "If you work hard, one day you may become a serving maid and get to see the king."

One day.

I saw him sooner than that. I sank into my straw that night as the clocks struck eleven. I dozed a little. I heard the bells chime midnight.

That was when guards came for me. They came quietly with a lantern that barely lit the bat-black night.

One of the men, the tall one, pressed a hand over my mouth as a sign that I should make no sound.

The horses stirred in the stable below as I groped my way down the stairs into the freezing courtyard.

We entered the kitchen into air that was thick with stale food and smoky smells. The guard opened the lantern and led me up the stairs.

I was so tired I could hardly drag myself on. At last, we came to the massive doors that led into the great hall.

The room was warmed by a log fire that lit the room, too. The high, carved thrones were empty. But a man in a dressing gown sat in front of the fire and smiled a thin-lipped smile into the flames.

The tall guard spoke for the first time. "Your Grace? We've brought you the girl."

The man turned and waved a hand for the guards to leave. He grinned at me.

His teeth were a little black with rot. It wasn't a pleasant smile. "Come in, Eleanor, and warm yourself."

I dropped a low curtsy to Henry Tudor, King Henry VII of England. "Thank you, Your Grace," I said humbly.

He gave a short laugh. "Eleanor, my dearest niece. You must call me Uncle Henry!"

"How was your work in the kitchen?" King Henry asked.

"It nearly killed me, Uncle," I groaned.

I stretched and yawned wearily as I sat on a bench at the fireplace.

He nodded. "But no one suspects you? They all believe you're just a common serving girl?"

"Yes, Uncle, we've fooled them," I said. "No one could guess I'm Lady Eleanor Tudor of Pembroke in Wales."

"Good," he said, rubbing his hands in front of the fire. "Then you are the perfect spy. We Tudors must stick together. I can trust no one outside of my family. There are thousands who want me dead, you know. Dead as a duck's toenail!"

The king stroked the fur collar on his gown, and the collar moved. It was a small brown monkey. It looked at me, then went back to sleep. "There are rebels and traitors everywhere."

"Yes, Uncle, I know," I said.

Mother had told me of the danger. If Henry Tudor lost the throne, then our family back in Wales would suffer, too. They might even kill us the way they killed the princes in the Tower.

"Have you met Lambert 'Simple' Simnel?"

"Yes, Uncle."

"Did your mother tell you about him?"

"Yes, Uncle. Lambert says he's Prince Edward, but really he's an organ-maker's son from Oxford," I said. "The real Prince Edward is still locked in the Tower of London."

The king stroked his long chin. "He may look a little bit like Prince Edward. The trouble is, my enemies put a crown on Lambert's head and sent an army from Ireland to kill me!"

"But you won the battle and captured Lambert. You made him a kitchen boy to show what a good, kind king you are," I said.

"I did! There are still people who think Simple Simnel could take my throne. There's only one person who knows for sure who that boy in the kitchen really is … and that's the boy in the kitchen!"

My uncle was quivering with so much rage the monkey on his shoulder stirred.

"Now he's afraid, so he says he's not Edward. First he is—then he isn't. What's the truth?"

"I'll find out for you, Uncle," I promised. "What will you do if he is the true king?"

Uncle Henry blinked in surprise. "Why, have him killed, of course!"

The Cruel Cook

I worked in the kitchen until my fingers bled and my nails cracked.

My fair skin was roasted when I turned the meat over the fire and my bare feet were black with the dirt.

When I got home to Wales, I'd make sure servants had a better life than this.

On the fourth day, I struggled to carry a leather bucket of water from the well.

Fat Cook told me to hurry and swung his boot at my backside. I stumbled and spilled the water.

"Stupid girl," he snarled. "You'll have to do it all over again!"

I sighed, picked up the empty bucket, and trudged back to the well. Lambert helped me carry it back to the door.

"He's a bully," Lambert said.

"Then I'll have to teach him a lesson," I snapped.

Lambert stopped and looked at me carefully. "You're a kitchen maid—what can you do?"

I almost blurted, "The king is my uncle, and I can have Cook executed with his own meat-ax!" But I had to keep my secret. I still had to fool Lambert into telling me the truth. I said, "There is some yellow-dock plant in the pantry, isn't there?"

Lambert nodded.

"Can we get some?"

"It's locked by Cook," he said, "but I can open locked doors."

I grinned. "How did you learn that?"

"My father made organs in Oxford, and I helped with the locks on the lid. I know all about them."

I stopped in the freezing yard. "I thought your father was the Duke of Clarence and you were the true king?"

Lambert laughed. "That's right. But I was switched when I was a baby to save me from being done away with. The organ-maker's son was brought up as Edward … and I was brought up as the organ-maker's son! I still think of him as my father. The rebels knew that—but they died in the battle."

"But does Unc—er... King Henry know that?"

"No! If he did, he'd execute me. I'm a bit simple—but I'm not crazy. Of course, no one knows the truth," he laughed.

"Except me," I said.

"Except you— and you're not going to tell the king, are you?"

The kitchen was quiet. The servants watched us, open-mouthed.

Cook had locked himself in the pantry for lunch. I put my ear to the door and heard him snore. I stood aside and let Lambert work on the lock with a knife. In a few moments it clicked open.

The leather hinge creaked. I peered around the door. Cook snored on. His wine cup sat on the bench beside him.

The pantry was full of cooked meats and pastries, cheeses and bread, wine, honey, and herbs. It was like a treasure chest. I passed a large cheese out to the servants, and they hurried to a corner to carve it and eat it before Cook woke up.

The stone jar of yellow-dock leaves scraped as I lifted it from the shelf. Cook stirred. He snorted. He belched. He smiled in his sleep.

I rubbed the leaves between my hands and let the powder fall into his wine cup.

Lambert gasped. "But …"

"Shhhh!"

I put more powder in the cup.

"But he'll …"

"Shhhh!"

I put the empty jar back on the shelf. We crept out, and Lambert locked the door.

We waited.

An hour later, Cook came out, red-faced and shouting orders. We scuttled around the kitchen like the rats in my hayloft, making dinner for the royal family and their guests.

King Henry was tight with his money, but he always put on a good feast when he had guests. We baked a fish pie, roasted pheasants and a baby pig, boiled dishes of peas, and made cups of rose-flavored custard. Six o'clock chimed. Dinner was ready to serve.

Cook clutched his fat gut—that was the yellow-dock powder starting to work.

Lambert chewed a knuckle nervously. "Yellow-dock makes you run to the john," he whimpered.

"Yes, Cook will need the toilet very soon— and for a long time," I said. "That's my revenge for him kicking me."

Cook rubbed his gut and tried to smile.

"A feast fit for a king!" he cried. "I will lead the way," he told the serving men. "King Henry can tell me to my face how great I am!" He turned on us. "You stay here and start clearing up, or I'll whip you raw!"

But when he left, we followed the procession to the great hall.

Greedy Guts

Lambert and I looked through a crack in the door. Uncle Henry sat at the top table with his guests from France. Their rich robes of crimson and gold, peacock blue and leaf green, were as fine as the ones I'd left at home.

And now that I had Lambert's secret, I could set off for Wales very soon. But first, there was the business of Cook to finish.

"My lords!" Cook cried.

Silence fell on the great hall. Suddenly the smile slid from his face like jelly off a plate. He clutched his gut and let out the loudest and most disgusting sound I have ever heard.

Pfffffthththththth-tttttttt

"Sorry, Your Grace!" he groaned and repeated the sound.

Pfffththththththth-tttttttt

"Oh, I need the john!" he cried and rushed to the door at the side of the hall.

"Not there!" Uncle Henry called.

Too late. Cook tore open the toilet door.

The queen, who was in there at the time, screamed, "Help, guards! Help!"

The guards drew their swords and rushed to grab Cook. He barged past them and ran for the main door where we were hiding.

"Don't arrest me yet!" he wailed as he rushed past us, smelling like a sewer drain and his guts gurgling like one, too.

"I need the **toilet!**"

Cook was fat but ran like a greyhound. The guards ran faster. They caught him when he reached the door to the toilet in the west tower.

"Please! Please! Please …

Pfffththththththth-tttttttt

just let me go to the …

Pfffththththththth-*ttttttt* …

toilet."

The guards grabbed him and dragged him
toward the dungeon.

"Oh, no-o-o-o-o!" Cook sobbed. "Now
look what you've made me *do-o-o-o-o-o!"*

It was the last I saw of him. Of course, I wasn't around for much longer. Cook would be fired when he was finally released. I stayed long enough to see how happy Lambert and the servants were with their new cook. Long enough to say goodbye to Lambert Simnel—"traitor."

"Now that Cook's gone, I'm really happy, Ellie," he said.

"As happy as a prince?" I asked.

"Happier," he laughed.

I never told him that I was a Tudor—his deadliest enemy.

That evening, I went to my hayloft and packed my bundle of clothes.

All I wanted was a warm bath, my own bed, and my Welsh home. But before I left, I had to tell Uncle Henry the truth about Lambert Simnel.

The Terrible Truth

The guards came for me as midnight chimed.

"Well, Eleanor? Have you learned the truth?" my uncle asked me as he sat before the fire. The monkey turned its head as if it were waiting for my answer.

"I have," I said.

"Is the boy Lambert Simnel or is he Prince Edward?" he asked.

"Is your executioner's ax sharp?" I asked.

Uncle licked his thin lips. "It is."

I smiled. "A pity. He won't be needing it. Lambert Simnel is … Lambert Simnel. The man he calls father is an Oxford organ-maker."

Well? I was telling the truth, wasn't I?

"He's a harmless boy," I said.

"Thank you, Eleanor. The boy can live. The world can see we Tudors are firm, but fair," he said.

I thought of Cook in the dungeon. "Yes, Uncle Henry. The world can see it doesn't pay to tangle with a Tudor."

Afterword: Lambert's Story

The Prince, the Cook, and the Cunning King is a story based on real people and events in Tudor times in England.

Edward, Earl of Warwick, had more right to be king of England than Henry Tudor. So Henry Tudor locked Edward in the Tower of London, then had himself crowned Henry VII.

Henry's enemies found 11-year-old Lambert Simnel in Oxford and thought he looked a lot like the imprisoned prince. They taught him to act like Prince Edward, then they took him to Ireland where they raised an army. They planned to invade England, beat Henry in battle, and put Lambert on the throne—though of course, they would really run the country for him.

But, when they met Henry's army at the Battle of Stoke Field in 1487, they were beaten. Lambert was taken prisoner, and Henry sent him to work in his castle kitchens.

The *real* Prince Edward stayed in the Tower of London. Twelve years later, there was a plot to free Prince Edward from the Tower. King Henry did not want to take any chances. He had the real Edward executed.

Lambert Simnel became a loyal servant and was released from kitchen work. He took a job looking after the king's falcons and was still doing that when Henry VII's son, Henry VIII, came to the throne.

There is just a chance that Edward and Lambert were switched as babies. (Many people in England believed that at the time.) If Lambert knew that then, as in the story, he kept quiet. Sensible. After all … it doesn't pay to tangle with a Tudor!

Look for all the

Historical Tales

by best-selling author Terry Deary